CLASS PET

THE HAMSTER IN OUR CLASS

Mitchell Lane
PUBLISHERS

Printing   1   2   3   4   5   6   7   8   9

The Fish in Our Class
The Frog in Our Class
The Hamster in Our Class
The Turtle in Our Class

Library of Congress Cataloging-in-Publication Data applied for.

ISBN: 9781584159803
eBook ISBN: 9781612281490

ABOUT THE AUTHOR: Children's book writer Kathleen Tracy lives in Southern California with her beloved dogs and an African gray parrot.

PLB

CLASS PET

RANDY'S CORNER

THE HAMSTER IN OUR CLASS

KATHLEEN TRACY

Mitchell Lane
PUBLISHERS
P.O. Box 196
Hockessin, Delaware 19707
Visit us on the web: www.mitchelllane.com

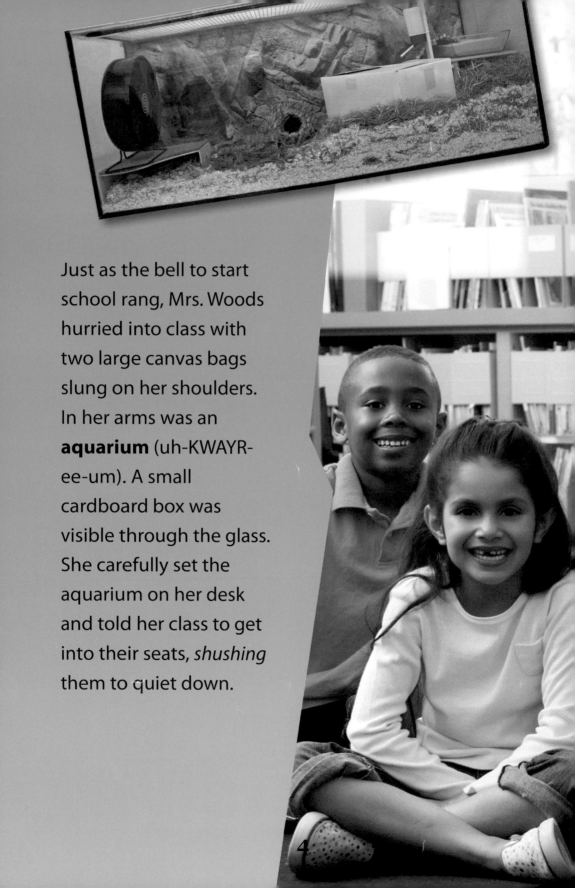

Just as the bell to start school rang, Mrs. Woods hurried into class with two large canvas bags slung on her shoulders. In her arms was an **aquarium** (uh-KWAYR-ee-um). A small cardboard box was visible through the glass. She carefully set the aquarium on her desk and told her class to get into their seats, *shushing* them to quiet down.

"Okay, everyone, I want to introduce you to the newest member of our class."

Mrs. Woods reached into the aquarium and opened the top of the box. Everyone sat forward, watching excitedly. The box jiggled and two tiny paws grabbed on to the edge, followed by a head rising out of the box.

"It's a hamster!" Paula laughed.

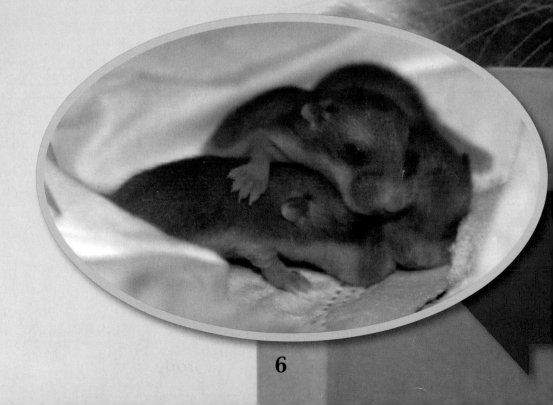

Hamsters are **rodents** [ROH-dents], a kind of mammal. Male hamsters are called bucks, and females are called does. A group of hamsters is called a horde.

"That's right," said Mrs. Woods. "Meet Hamlet, our new class pet." She gently tilted the box and Hamlet crawled out. His round black eyes stared at the class.

UNITED
STATES

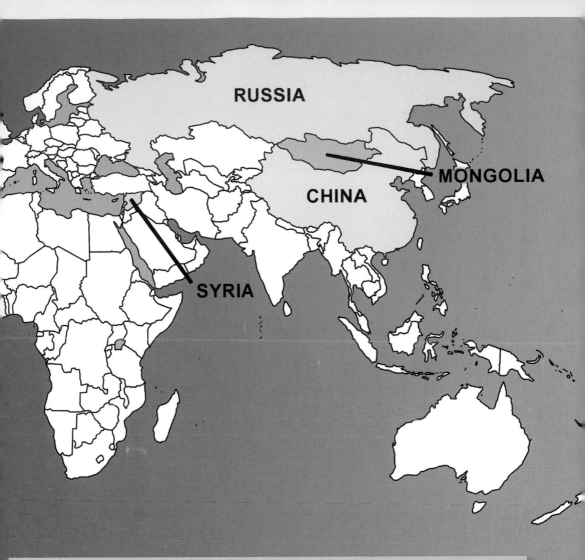

RUSSIA

CHINA

MONGOLIA

SYRIA

"I have hamsters at home," Cindy said. "They are a lot smaller than Hamlet."

"That's because there are different types of hamsters. Hamlet is a Syrian [SEE-ree-un] hamster." Mrs. Woods walked to the map of the world and pointed. "His relatives come from Syria in the Middle East, right here."

Hamsters are crepuscular [kreh-PUS-kyoo-lur], which means they are most active at dusk and at dawn.

She explained that Syrian hamsters are also called teddy bear or golden hamsters, "because of their fur color, and they're kind of plump." She spun the globe and

pointed to a spot in Asia. "There are also Chinese hamsters. They are small and come from the desert in northern China and Mongolia. Dwarf hamsters live in a grassy area called the **steppes** in Russia." She pointed again at the map.

Hamsters normally give birth to 8 to 10 babies, called pups, at a time. Syrian hamsters have been known to have up to 20 pups at once!

"Won't Hamlet get lonely not having another hamster to play with?" Randy asked.

"No. Syrian hamsters need to live alone. He would fight another hamster. Dwarf hamsters like having company. So do Chinese hamsters. But all hamsters like having a warm comfortable home. Who wants to help set up Hamlet's house?"

A hamster's front teeth are called incisors (in-SY-zors). They never stop growing. To keep their teeth filed down, let them gnaw on a dog biscuit.

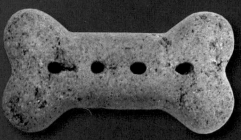

Paula got his food ready. She filled his bowl with hamster mix. It contained corn, cereal, alfalfa, and different types of seeds such as sunflower, flax, and pumpkin seeds.

"Hamsters also like fruit and fresh veggies like carrots," Mrs. Woods mentioned. "We just have to be careful not to overfeed him."

Randy, Cindy, and the rest of the students helped Mrs. Woods put Hamlet's home together. The bottom was the aquarium. Connected to the top was a wire cage. They attached platforms to the cage wires and added a ladder so that Hamlet could climb up and down.

Hamsters can carry enough food in their cheek pouches to equal half their body weight.

"This cage looks funny," Celeste said.

"It's called a **hybrid** cage," explained Mrs. Woods. "Hamsters need a lot of space. They like to have one area to sleep in, one to use as a bathroom, and one where they can keep their food. Hamlet can stay warm in the aquarium when he sleeps, but he still gets lots of fresh air."

They added an exercise wheel, put in his food, and attached a water bottle.

In the wild, hamsters live in burrows.

"The last thing he needs," said Mrs. Woods, "is a place to sleep." She placed a handful of dried grass, some straw, and some plain tissue in the aquarium. Hamlet immediately set about making a bed.

Mrs. Woods carefully carried the hybrid cage to a table in the back of the room, away from the window so that Hamlet would not be in direct sunlight.

Wear gloves until your hamster is comfortable being held. He might bite if startled.

Although you may find wood chips sold as hamster bedding, be sure not to use cedar or pine chips. These types of wood can harm your pet.

The class agreed to take turns giving Hamlet fresh food and water every day. On Fridays, they would clean his cage and fill his feeder so that he'd have enough food over the weekend.

Hamlet yawned, curled into a ball, and went to sleep. He seemed happy in his new home.

GERBILS VS HAMSTERS

Your classroom may want to have gerbils instead of a hamster. While these two types of pets have a lot in common, here are some differences that might help you choose the better pet for your class:

HAMSTERS

- Hamsters are awake at dawn and dusk. They sleep all day.
- Hamsters run on exercise wheels but do not have a lot of energy.
- Hamsters like to live alone. Adults will fight other hamsters, even young ones.
- Hamsters are more likely to bite their owners.
- Hamster cages need to be cleaned more often than gerbil cages.
- Hamsters have short, stubby bare tails.

GERBILS

- Gerbils do not sleep all day. They take short naps instead.
- Gerbils are fun to watch because they have a lot of energy.
- Gerbils like to live in pairs. They take good care of their babies.
- Gerbils that have been handled from a young age rarely bite.
- Gerbils are desert animals. Their cages stay clean longer than hamster cages.
- Gerbils have long tails with a furry tuft at the end.

Books

Newcomb, Rain. *Is My Hamster Wild? The Secret Lives of Hamsters, Gerbils & Guinea Pigs.* Asheville, NC: Lark Books, 2008.

Richardson, Alan, and Adele Faber. *Caring for Your Hamster.* Mankato, MN: Capstone Press, 2006.

Sabates, Berta Garcia, and Merce Segarra. *Let's Take Care of Our New Hamster.* Hauppauge, NY: Barron's Educational Series, 2008.

Works Consulted

ASPCA, Hamster Care
    http://www.aspca.org/pet-care/small-pet-care/hamster-care.html

Drs. Foster & Smith, Hamster Fun Facts
    http://www.drsfostersmith.com/pic/article.cfm?aid=1276

The Humane Society, Hamsters
    http://www.humanesociety.org/animals/hamsters/

GLOSSARY

aquarium (uh-KWAYR-ee-um)—A glass or plastic box designed to hold fish or other animals.

burrow (BUR-oh)—A hole or tunnel dug into the ground and used as a home.

crepuscular (kreh-PUS-kyoo-lur)—Active at dusk and dawn.

hybrid (HY-brid)—Something made by crossing or combining two different things.

incisors (in-SY-zors)—A hamster's front teeth.

rodent (ROH-dent)—A mammal that has two pairs of continuously growing teeth; includes mice and squirrels.

steppes (STEPS)—A dry, grassy plain found in Siberia, an area in Russia.